William and the White Elephants and Other Stories

Richmal Crompton, who wrote the original *Just William* stories, was born in Lancashire in 1890. The first story about William Brown appeared in *Home* magazine in 1919, and the first collection of William stories was published in book form three years later. In all, thirty-eight William books were published, the last one in 1970, after Richmal Crompton's death.

Martin Jarvis, who has adapted the stories in this book for younger readers, first discovered *Just William* when he was nine years old. He made his first adaptation of a William story for BBC radio in 1973 and since then his broadcast readings have become classics in their own right. BBC Worldwide have released nearly a hundred William stories on audio cassette and for these international best-sellers Martin has received a Gold Disc and the British Talkies Award. An award-winning actor, Martin has also appeared in numerous stage plays, television series and films.

All *Meet Just William* titles can be ordered at
your local bookshop or are available by post
from Book Service by Post (tel: 01624 675137).

Meet
Just William

William and the White Elephants and Other Stories

Adapted from Richmal Crompton's
original stories by Martin Jarvis

Illustrated by Tony Ross

MACMILLAN CHILDREN'S BOOKS

First published 2000 by Macmillan Children's Books
a division of Macmillan Publishers Limited
20 New Wharf Road, London N1 9RR
Basingstoke and Oxford
www.panmacmillan.com

Associated companies throughout the world

ISBN 0 330 39210 7

3 5 7 9 8 6 4 2

A CIP catalogue record for this book is available from
the British Library.

Typeset by SX Composing DTP, Rayleigh, Essex
Printed and bound in Great Britain by Mackays of Chatham plc, Kent

Contents

Dear Reader

Ullo. I'm William Brown. Spect you've heard of me an' my dog Jumble cause we're jolly famous on account of all the adventures wot me an' my friends the Outlaws have.

Me an' the Outlaws try an' avoid our famlies cause they don' unnerstan' us. Specially my big brother Robert an' my rotten sister Ethel. She's awful. An' my parents are really hartless. Y'know, my father stops my pocket-money for no reason at all, an' my mother never lets me keep pet rats or anythin'.

It's jolly hard bein' an Outlaw an' havin' adventures when no one unnerstan's you, I can tell you.

You can read all about me, if you like, in this excitin' an' speshul new collexion of all my fav'rite stories. I hope you have a jolly gud time readin' 'em.

Yours truly

William Brown

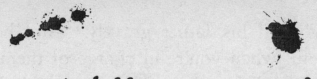

William and the White Elephants

"William," said Mrs Brown to her younger son, "as Robert will be away, I think it would be rather nice if you helped me on my stall at the Conservative Fête."

"What sort of a stall you goin' to have?" said William.

"A White Elephant stall," said Mrs Brown.

William showed signs of animation. "And where you goin' to gettem?" he said.

"Oh, people will give them," said Mrs Brown vaguely.

"*Crumbs*!" said William.

"You must be very careful with them,

William," said his father gravely. "And be very careful when you're in charge of them. They're difficult beasts to handle."

"Don't tease him, dear," said Mrs Brown, to her husband; and to William, "white elephants, dear, are things you don't need."

"I know," said William. "I know *I* don't need 'em, but I s'pose some people do, or you won't be sellin' 'em."

The subsequent discovery of the real meaning of the term "White Elephant" filled William with such disgust that he announced that nothing would now induce him to attend the Fête in any capacity whatsoever.

But when the day arrived William had relented. After all there was something thrilling about serving at a stall.

The White Elephant stall contained the usual medley of battered household goods, unwanted Christmas presents and old clothes.

Mrs Brown stood, placid and serene, behind it. William stood at the side of it, surveying it scornfully.

The other Outlaws, who had no official positions, were watching him from a distance.

His mother turned to him and said, "I won't be a second away, William, just keep an eye on things," and departed.

That was splendid. He moved right to the centre of the stall.

A woman came up to the stall and examined a black coat lying across the corner of it.

"You can have that for a shilling," said William generously.

He looked at the Outlaws from the corner of his eye, hoping that they noticed him left thus in sole charge, fixing prices, selling goods, and generally directing affairs.

The woman handed him a shilling and disappeared with the coat into the crowd.

Soon his mother returned and he moved to the side of the stall.

Then Mrs Monks, the Vicar's wife, came up. She looked about the stall anxiously, then said to William's mother, "I thought I'd put my coat down just here for a few minutes, dear. You haven't seen it, have you? I put it just here. It's a black one."

William's mother joined in the search.

Over William's face stole a look of blank horror.

"Perhaps someone's just carried it in for you," said Mrs Brown.

"I'll go and see," said the Vicar's wife.

William (very quietly) joined Ginger, Henry and Douglas, who had watched the denouement open-mouthed.

"You won't half catch it," said Douglas cheerfully, "they'll be sure to find out who did it."

"Tell you what," said Ginger, "let's go an' get it back."

A cursory examination of the crowd who thronged the Vicarage garden revealed no black coat to the anxious Outlaws.

They went to the gate and looked up and down the road.

"*There* she is," said Ginger suddenly, "walkin' down the road in it – *cheek*!"

The figure of a woman wearing a black coat could be seen a few hundred yards down the road. The Outlaws set off in pursuit.

They slowed down.

She went in at the gate of a small house.

The Outlaws clustered round the gate, gazing at the front door as it closed behind her.

"Well, we've got to get it back," said William.

He swaggered up the path and rang the bell violently. A maid opened the door. William cleared his throat nervously. "Scuse me, if it's not troublin' you too much—"

"Now, then," said the girl sharply, "none of your sauce."

William redoubled his already exaggerated courtesy. "Scuse me," he said, "but a lady's jus' come into this house wearin' a white elephant—"

He was outraged to receive a sudden smack, accompanied by a, "Get out, you saucy little 'ound," and the slamming of the front door in his face.

William rejoined his giggling friends.

"I'll go'n have a try, shall I?" said Ginger.

"All right," said William.

And Ginger, imitating William's swagger, walked up the front door and knocked. The haughty housemaid opened the door.

"G'd afternoon," said Ginger with a courteous smile. "Scuse me, but will you kin'ly tell the lady what's jus' come in here wearin' a black coat that I'll give her one an' six for it an'—"

Ginger also received a smack that sent him rolling halfway down the drive, and the door was slammed in his face.

An informal meeting was then held to consider their next step.

They went round to the side gate where they crouched in the bushes watching the redoubtable William as he crept across the lawn up to a small open window. Breathlessly they watched him hoist himself up and swing his legs over the window sill.

No sooner had William found himself in the room, than he heard voices approaching the door. He dived beneath the round table in the middle of the room.

The lady whom the Outlaws had followed down the road – now divested of the fateful black coat – entered, followed by another more highly coloured lady.

"A *black* coat, did you say?" said the first lady.

William, beneath the table, pricked up his ears.

7

"Yes, if you can, Mrs Bute," said the highly coloured lady. "I only want it for tomorrow for the funeral."

"Certainly," said Mrs Bute. "I can lend you one with pleasure. It's in the hall. It's one I've only just bought . . ."

They went into the hall, and William gathered that the black coat was being displayed.

"Quite a bargain, wasn't it?" he heard Mrs Bute say.

Huh!

They returned – evidently with the coat.

"Thank you so much, my dear," said the highly coloured lady, "it's just what I wanted and *so* smart. What was it like at the Fête?" She was trying on the coat and examining herself in the mirror. "I must say, it *does* suit me."

"Oh, very dull," said Mrs Bute. "I came away before it was actually opened. Just got what I wanted and then came away."

The highly coloured lady sniffed.

"I must say that I was a bit *hurt* that they didn't ask me to give an entertainment. People have so often told me that no function about here is complete without one of my entertainments – and then not to ask me to entertain at the Conservative Fête."

Suddenly William knew who she was. She must be Miss Poll. He remembered now hearing his mother say only yesterday, "That dreadful Gertie Poll wants to give an entertainment at the Fête, and we're *determined* not to ask her. She's so *vulgar*. She'd cheapen

9

the whole thing . . ."

"Of course," said Mrs Bute. "Of course, dear, but . . . the coat will do, will it?"

"Very nicely, thank you," said Miss Poll. "Good afternoon, dear."

There followed the sound of the closing of the front door. William retreated through his open window and rejoined Douglas and Henry at the gate. Ginger had vanished.

"Quick," said William, "*she's* got it. We've gotter follow *her*. She's got it now."

At this minute Ginger reappeared. "There's another!" said Ginger. "There's *another* black coat hangin' up in the hall. I've been round an' looked through a little window an' *seen* it."

William said, "Well, I bet the one she took's the one, 'cause I heard her say, wasn't it a bargain. All right, you an' Douglas stay here, an' Henry 'n' me'll go after the other, an' I *bet* you ours is the right one."

Five minutes later William and Henry stood at Miss Poll's gate.

Then, boldly, William walked up to the front door and rang the bell. Apprehensively Henry followed him.

Miss Poll, wearing the black coat, for she had been trying it on, opened the door.

"G'afternoon, Miss Poll, please will you come to the Fête to give an entertainment?"

Miss Poll went rather red and simpered coyly. "You – you've been sent on a message, I suppose, little boy? I *thought* there must be some mistake . . . I *knew* that *really* they couldn't get on without me. They didn't send a note by you, I suppose?"

'No," said William quite truthfully.

She pouted. "Well, *that* I think is rather rude, don't you? Still, I mustn't keep the poor dears waiting. I'll be ready in a second."

Then Miss Poll underwent a short inward struggle which William watched breathlessly.

It was obvious that Miss Poll was torn between the joy of wearing the coat and the impropriety of wearing for a festal occasion a garment borrowed for a funeral. To William's relief the coat won the day and, putting on a smart hat with a very red feather, she joined them at the door.

William was tense. The next step would be to detach the coat from Miss Poll's person.

William had an idea, based on his not inconsiderable understanding of the female psyche. He looked Miss Poll up and down, and said, "Funny!"

"What's funny?" said Miss Poll sharply.

"Oh, nothin', only I've jus' remembered that I saw someone at the Fête in a coat *exactly* like that one what you've got on."

There was a silence and finally Miss Poll said, "It is a little hot, dear. If you would be so kind as to carry my coat—"

She took it off, revealing a dress that was very short and very diaphanous and very, very pink. She handed the coat to William.

William heaved a sigh of relief. They had reached the gate of the Vicarage now. They were only just in time . . .

William meant to thrust the coat into the arms of the Vicar's wife and escape as quickly as he could, leaving Miss Poll to her fate, but it happened that the local Member of Parliament's political agent had collected a large audience into the main tent, where the Member was to "say a few words" on the political situation.

The agent was hovering ready to tell him that his audience was awaiting him, when the contretemps occurred.

Miss Poll tripped airily up to the door of the tent in her pink, pink frock, peeped in, saw an audience with a vacant place in front of them and, skipping lightly in with a "*So* sorry to have kept you all waiting," leapt at once into her first item – an imitation of a tipsy land-lady.

The audience, very heavy and respectable, gaped at her, astounded. And when, a few minutes later the Member of Parliament, calm and dignified, appeared at the door of the tent he found Miss Gertie Poll prancing to and fro before his amazed audience, her pink, pink skirts held very high, announcing that she was Gilbert the Filbert, the colonel of the nuts.

The agent, looking over his shoulder, grew pale and loose-jawed. The Member turned to him. "What's all this?" he demanded.

The agent mopped his brow. "I – I – I've no idea, sir."

"Please put a stop to it," said the Member and added hastily, remembering that the tent was packed full of votes, "without any unpleasantness, of course."

But it would have taken more than a dozen political agents to stop Miss Gertie Poll in full flow of her repertoire. She went on for over an hour. She merely smiled bewitchingly at the agent whenever he tried to stop her without any unpleasantness, and when the Member himself appeared to take command of the situation, she blew him a kiss and he hastily retired.

Meanwhile William, triumphantly bearing

the black coat, made his way up to the Vicar's wife. He met Ginger and Douglas, also carrying a black coat and on the same mission.

"We got it out of her hall," said Douglas cheerfully. "I bet *ours* is the one."

"Well, come on an' see," said William, pushing his way up to the stall presided over by the Vicar's wife.

"Here's your coat, Mrs Monks. It was sold by mistake off the rubbish stall but we've got it back for you – me an' Henry."

Before the Vicar's wife could answer, a frantic messenger came up to her.

"What *shall* we do? Miss Poll's entertaining the tent, and the Member can't speak."

"Miss *Poll*!" gasped the Vicar's wife. "We never asked her."

"No, but she's *come* and she's singing all her *awful* songs and no one can stop her, and the Member can't speak."

The Vicar's wife, still absently nursing the coat that William had thrust into her arms, stared in front of her.

16

Then Ginger came up and thrust the second coat into her unprotesting arms. "Your coat, Mrs Monks," he said politely. "What we sold by mistake off the rubbish stall. Me an' Douglas have got it back for you."

They waited breathlessly to see which coat the Vicar's wife should claim as her own.

She looked down at her armful of coats as if she saw them for the first time.

"B-but, I got that coat back. The woman who bought it thought there must be some mistake and brought it to me. These aren't my coats."

Shrill strains of some strident music-hall ditty came from the tent. Then a woman pushed her way through the crowds, up to the Vicar's wife. It was Mrs Bute.

"Brought it here, they did," she panted. "Where is it? *Thieves*! Came into my hall bold as brass an' *took* it! . . . *There* it is!" She glared suspiciously at the Vicar's wife. "What've *you* got it for . . . *my* coat . . . I'd like to know. I'd—"

She tore it out of her arms and the other coat, too, fell to the ground.

"My *other* coat!" she screamed. "*Both* my coats! *Thieves* – that's what you are! *Thieves*!"

"Where are those boys?" said the Vicar's wife very faintly. But "those boys" had disappeared.

They were found, of course, and brought back. They were forced to give explanations. They were forced to apologise to all concerned, even to Miss Poll (who forgave them because her little show had gone off so well). They were sent home in disgrace.

William's father said later, "Well I warned you, William. I told you they were difficult beasts to manage. Of course, if you lose control of a whole herd of white elephants like that, they're bound to do some damage."

And William said disgustedly, "I'm just *sick* of white elephants and black coats. I'm going out to play Red Indians."

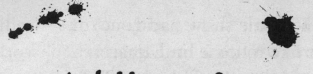

William Starts the Holidays

The Christmas holidays had arrived, and William and the other Outlaws – Ginger, Douglas and Henry – whooped their way home from school at the unusual hour of 11 a.m., to the unaffected dismay of their families.

"We've broke up!" yelled William, as he entered the hall and flung his satchel with a clatter upon the floor. "We've broke up!"

Mrs Brown came out of the morning-room, rather pale at this invasion of her usual morning quiet.

"I – I'd forgotten you were breaking up

today, William," she said. "You – you wouldn't like to do a little quiet school work here, would you, William dear, so as to keep your hand in for next term?"

"No thank you," said William, quite firmly. "I don't think it's fair on the other boys to go on workin' in the holidays."

While Mrs Brown was slowly recovering from this startling vision of William conscientiously refraining from holiday work for the sake of his classmates, she had an idea.

"William, it's so near Christmas time – wouldn't you like to be thinking out some little presents for people?"

"I've hardly any money," said William, "what with payin' for broken windows and things."

"Well," said Mrs Brown encouragingly, "it isn't the money you spend on them that people value. It's the thought behind it. I'm sure that with a little thought you could make some very nice presents for your relations and friends."

William considered the idea in silence for some minutes. Then he brightened. "All right," he said. "I'll go an' think upstairs."

A sense of peace stole over Mrs Brown.

Later, Robert and Ethel, William's grown-up brother and sister came to her in the morning-room to talk over their Christmas party.

"I say," said Robert, "I thought William was breaking up today."

"He is," said Mrs Brown, "he has broken

up. He came home about eleven o'clock."

"He's very quiet," said Ethel.

"Well," said Robert, "let's make the most of it."

Robert's and Ethel's Christmas party was a secret, only to be discussed when William was safely out of the way.

William, of course, knew that it was to take place, but so far they had managed to keep from him the fact that after supper there was going to be a short one-act play.

The shining lights of the local Dramatic Society (including Ethel and Robert) were going to take part. They kept this part of it particularly a secret from William, because William rather fancied himself as an actor.

They felt that if William knew that a one-act play was going to take place under his roof it would be practically impossible to protect the play from the devastating effects of William's interest in it.

They discussed the dancing and the supper and the play. Finally, Mrs Brown became a little anxious and said, "Ethel, dear, I wish you'd just run upstairs and have a look at William. He's so quiet. I hope he's not feeling ill or anything."

Visible gloom settled on the faces of Robert and Ethel at the mention of William. But Ethel went obediently from the room.

Moments later they heard a cry of "Mother!" from Ethel. They dashed upstairs. William, his face and hands and hair and clothes freely adorned with green paint, sat on his bedroom hearth rug, which had shared in the wholesale application of green paint.

On the hearth rug was a once-white straw hat of Ethel's, upon which William had obviously devoted much labour and green paint. He had, moreover, filled it with earth and planted in it a cyclamen from the greenhouse.

"Look," said Ethel. "My – my best hat!"

"Why, it's quite an ole hat, Ethel," said William, "I thought you must have about done with it."

"B-but, William," gasped Mrs Brown,

"what on earth have you been doing?"

"Well, you said *think* out Christmas presents, and *make* 'em, an' don' spend money on 'em, so I thought I'd start on Ethel's, an' I thought that I could paint one of Ethel's hats an' make it look like a kind of fancy plant pot with the paint from the shed, an' put a plant into it from the greenhouse. I thought it was rather a good idea," he ended modestly.

That was why, when William discovered

about the play, he was told that he was not to see it, either at rehearsals or on the evening of the party . . .

The night of the party arrived. William, shining with cleanliness, his hair brushed and greased, encased in his Eton suit, stood a little way from the rest of his family as guests began to arrive.

Some of the guests called out, "Hello, William." Others ignored him.

William tried to look bored and indifferent, but really he was looking forward to the dancing and the supper, and he meant to watch the play from the garden through the morning-room window.

The guests had all arrived. The music for the dancing had begun. William stood in the drawing-room, which had been "turned out" for the dance, and looked around him critically.

Slowly, he determined on the prettiest girl in the room and walked across to her, baring his teeth in what was meant to be an ingratiating smile.

Just as he was a few feet from her, Robert came up and claimed her, and they both moved off without looking at him. William's smile died away. He looked around the room again. All the girls seemed to be dancing now. No, there was one sitting by the window. She wasn't so bad, really, if you didn't look at her sideways.

William bared his teeth again (his jaws were aching by this time) and walked up to her.

"Excuse me—" he began. A man stepped up from the other side.

"Shall we?" he said to the girl, and off they went. William frowned and went with scornful dignity from the room. He went to the side door and looked out into the night. Ginger, Douglas and Henry were coming cautiously up the path. Whenever any of the Outlaws' families gave a party, the Outlaws would be there – uninvited, generally in the garden – keeping a friendly eye on the affair through the windows.

"Hello. We thought p'raps you'd be dancing," said Ginger.

"Oh, I got a bit tired of dancing," said William airily, "an' I came out to get cool. Come an' have a look at the supper."

They crept through the side door and into the dining-room. There William proudly pointed to the long trestle table, resplendent with food, including ices and fruit and trifles and jellies of every kind.

The Outlaws licked their lips. "Crumbs!" they gasped.

Suddenly there came the sound of the opening of the drawing-room door, and an influx of guests into the hall.

"Get under the table, quick!" said William.

So the Outlaws got under the table – quick.

The guests entered. They sat round the table. William was right at the corner, next to a tall thin young man, so the tall thin young man had to hand the dishes to William and keep him supplied. He tried at first to talk to William, but found this difficult.

"I suppose you've broken up?" he said.

"Yes," said William, his voice and face equally devoid of expression.

"Do you like the holidays?"

"Yes," said William in the same tone of voice.

"Are you fond of lessons?"

"No."

"I expect you're looking forward to Christmas."

William, considering this remark beneath

contempt, vouchsafed no answer. The tall thin young man, crushed, transferred his attention to the lady on the other side of him.

Now William was painfully conscious of the presence of Ginger, Henry and Douglas beneath the table. He could not eat in comfort with Ginger, Douglas and Henry so cramped and uncomfortable and hungry. He took two bites at the large sausage roll with which the tall thin young man had supplied him, then, looking dreamily at the opposite wall, slipped his hand under the table.

There another hand, grateful and unseen, promptly relieved him of the rest of the sausage roll. His plate was empty.

The tall thin young man looked at it. Then he looked at William. William met his eyes with an aggressive stare.

The tall thin young man looked at William's plate again. It was true. This child really had consumed a large sausage roll in less than ten seconds. He then took the whole dish of sausage rolls, put them just in front of

William, and turned to continue his conversation with his other neighbour.

This was just what William wanted. He took a roll on to his plate and looked around. With a lightning movement he transferred the roll to his knee and held it out beneath the table.

The unseen recipient grabbed it eagerly. William did the same with a second, a third, a fourth. He grew reckless. He put down a fifth, a sixth, a seventh. There were three more on the dish. One – two – three – then he turned his aggressive stare upon the tall thin young man.

As though hypnotised by the stare, the tall thin young man turned slowly to William. He looked at the empty plate and the empty dish in front of William and his jaw dropped open weakly. He tried to say, "And what can I pass you now?" But he couldn't. Words wouldn't come. The sight of that enormous empty dish had broken his nerve.

Just then a diversion occurred. A friend of Ethel's, sitting almost opposite, had slipped off her shoe under the table, and a few minutes later she made a large circular sweep in search of it with her stockinged foot and just caught Ginger on the neck where he was most ticklish.

Ginger dropped his half-eaten sausage roll and gave a loud yell. A sudden tense silence fell over the table.

Then the girl gave an embarrassed little giggle. "I'm afraid I kicked your dog – or your

cat – or something," she said.

She lifted up the tablecloth and grew pale. "It's boys," she said in a breathless whisper, "ever so many of them!"

It was half an hour later. Ginger, Douglas and Henry had been ignominiously ejected. William had been despatched to spend the rest of the evening in his bedroom.

The one-act play was being performed in the morning-room, and William had commanded his Outlaws to bring him some food from the dining-room. The Outlaws returned very quickly to beneath William's window.

"William," called Ginger excitedly, "There's a burglar in the dinin' room."

In less than a minute, William had joined the Outlaws outside the dining-room window. Yes, there he was, a real burglar in dingy clothes, a cap pulled low over his eyes, his bag of tools and a half-filled sack by him. He was standing at the sideboard drinking a whisky and soda.

"We'd better go'n tell your father," said Douglas.

"No, we'll catch him ourselves," said William.

There was an enormous curtain in a box upstairs. It would do nicely to catch the burglar in. In less than a minute, William returned with it.

The Outlaws crept into the dining-room silently and, stealing up behind the burglar, enveloped their prey, just as he was in the act of pouring out some more whisky.

He was taken completely by surprise and fell forward into a mass of all-enveloping green serge. He tried to regain his footing and failed. In his green serge covering he was being dragged somewhere. He shouted.

It happened that in the morning-room Ethel, in her capacity of heroine, had just finished singing a song, which was greeted with frenzied applause by her loyal guests. The applause drowned the burglar's shouts.

Douglas flung open the French windows

and the Outlaws dragged their victim out into the night across the lawn.

They hoisted the large curtain, which still contained its struggling inhabitant, into the greenhouse, shut the door and turned the key. William was still rent by the pangs of hunger.

"He's all right for a bit," he said. "He can't get out. Let's take a bit of food upstairs first. We can tell 'em after."

The Outlaws approved of this, and in a few minutes they were sitting on the floor of William's bedroom munching happily and discussing their capture.

Suddenly Ginger pricked up his ears.

"Seems a sort of noise going on downstairs," he said.

Very softly, the Outlaws crept out on to the landing. Everyone seemed to be bustling about, and talking excitedly.

"Do be quiet a minute while I ring up his mother," said Ethel's voice, distraught and tearful. "Hello – hello – is that Mrs Langley? Has Harold come home? *Hasn't* he? No, he's completely disappeared – we got to the point in the play where he comes on – just after my song, you know, and I waited and *waited* and he never came, and I had to leave the stage without finishing the scene. My nerves had absolutely all gone. We couldn't go on without him. He was playing the burglar, you know. It's quite spoilt the party, of course, and *ruined* the play."

She was interrupted by Mrs Brown's voice, high and hysterical.

"Oh, Ethel, do fetch your father. It's too dark to see anything – but someone's breaking all the glass in the greenhouse."

The entire party sallied out excitedly into the garden. The Outlaws, acting with great presence of mind, fled to their several homes.

And William got into bed, and went to sleep. He went to sleep with almost incredible rapidity. When his family entered his bedroom a few minutes later, demanding an explanation, William lay determinedly and unwakably asleep.

"Oh, don't wake him," pleaded Mrs Brown. "It's so bad for children to be startled out of their sleep."

"Sleep!" said Robert sarcastically. "Well, I don't mind. It can wait till tomorrow for all I care. The party's ruined anyway."

Fortunately, they did not look under the bed, or they would have seen a large plate piled with appetising dainties.

They went away with threatening murmurs in which the word "tomorrow" figured largely. When they had gone, William got out of bed with great caution and sat in the darkness munching iced cakes.

That sleep idea had been jolly good. Of course, he knew it couldn't go on indefinitely. He'd have to wake up tomorrow, but tomorrow was tomorrow, and when tonight holds an entire plate of iced cakes (many of them with layers of real cream inside), tomorrow is hardly worth serious consideration . . .

The Best-Laid Plans

"She's a real Botticelli," said the young man dreamily, as he watched the figure of William's sister, Ethel, disappearing into the distance.

William glared at him. "Bottled cherry yourself!" he said indignantly. "She can't help havin' red hair, can she? No more'n you can help havin' – havin' big ears."

The young man did not resent the insult. He did not even hear it. His eyes were still fixed upon the slim figure in the distance. The young man – James French by name – had met Ethel at a party and had succumbed to her charm. Lacking courage to pursue the acquaintance, he had cultivated the friendship of her small brother, under a quite erroneous impression that this would win him Ethel's good graces.

"What would you like most in the world?" he said suddenly, leaning forward from his seat on top of the gate. "Suppose someone let you choose."

"White rats," said William, without a moment's hesitation.

The young man was plunged into deep thought. "I've thought of a way," he said at last. "Yes. This is my idea."

The young man talked earnestly. William's mouth opened wide. The words "white rats" were repeated frequently.

Finally William nodded his head. "I s'pose you're barmy on her," he said, "like what folks are in books. I want 'em with long tails, mind."

The next morning William assumed an

expression of shining virtue.

"You goin' shoppin' this mornin'?" he enquired politely of Ethel.

"You know I am," said Ethel shortly.

"Shall I come with you to carry parcels an' things?" said William unctuously.

Ethel looked at him with sudden suspicion.

"What do you want? I'm not going to buy you anything."

William looked pained. "I don't want anything. I jus' want to *help* you. I jus' want to carry your parcels for you. I – I jus' don't want you to get *tired*, that's all."

"All right." Ethel was still suspicious. "You can come and you can carry parcels, but you won't get a penny out of me."

They walked down together to the shops, and William meekly allowed himself to be laden with many parcels. Ethel's grim suspicion became bewilderment as he passed the toyshop without a glance. In his imagination he was already teaching complicated tricks to a pair of white rats.

"It's – it's awfully decent of you, William,"
said Ethel at last. "Do you feel all right? I
mean, you don't feel ill or anything, do you?"

"No," he said absently, then corrected himself hastily. "At least, not *jus'* now. I feel as if I
might not feel all right soon, but I don't know."

Ethel looked anxious. "Let's get home
quickly. What have you been eating?"

"Nothing," said William. "I'm all right jus'
now."

They walked in silence till they had left the

main road behind and had turned off to the country road that led to William's house. Then, slowly and deliberately, still clasping his burden of parcels, William sat down on the ground.

"I can't walk any more, Ethel," he said, turning his healthy countenance up to her. "I'm took ill sudden."

She looked down at him impatiently.

"Don't be absurd, William. Get up."

"I'm not absurd," he said firmly. "I'm took ill."

"Where do you feel ill?"

"All over," he said guardedly. "I'm took too ill to walk."

She looked round anxiously.

"Oh, what *are* we going to do? It's a quarter of a mile home!"

At that moment there appeared the figure of a tall young man. He drew nearer and raised his hat.

"Anything wrong, Miss Brown?" he said, blushing deeply.

"Just *look* at William! He says he can't walk, and goodness knows what we're going to do."

The young man bent over William, but avoided meeting his eyes. "You feeling ill, my little man?" hc said cheerfully.

"Huh!" snorted William. "That's a nice thing for *you* to ask when you know you—"

"Yes, all right," he said hastily. "Well, let's see what we can do. Could you get on my back, and then I can carry you home? Give me your parcels. That's right. No, Miss Brown. I *insist* on carrying the parcels. I couldn't *dream* of allowing you. Now, William, are we ready?"

William clung on behind, and they set off, rather slowly, down the road.

Ethel was overcome with gratitude. "It *is* kind of you, Mr French. I don't know what we should have done without you. I do hope he's not fearfully heavy; and I do hope he's not beginning anything infectious."

Mr French stumbled along unsteadily. "Oh,

no," he panted. "Don't mention it – don't mention it. It's a pleasure – really it is. No, he isn't a bit heavy. Not a bit. I'm so glad I happened to come by."

The curious little group eventually arrived at the Browns' house.

Mrs Brown saw them from the window and ran to the door. "Oh dear!" she said. "You've run over him on your motorcycle."

Ethel interrupted indignantly. "Why, Mother, Mr French has been so kind. I can't think what I'd have done without him. William was taken ill and couldn't walk, and Mr French has carried him all the way from the other end of the road, on his back."

"Oh, I'm *so* sorry! How very kind of you, Mr French. Do come in and stay to lunch. William, go upstairs to bed at once, and I'll ring up Dr Ware."

"No," said William firmly. "I'm all right now. Honest I am."

"What do you think, Mr French?" said Mrs Brown anxiously.

Both Mrs Brown and Ethel turned to him as to an oracle.

"Oh – er – well," he said nervously. "He *looks* all right, doesn't he? I – er – wouldn't bother. Just – er – don't worry him with questions. I – er – think it's best to – let him forget it," he ended weakly.

"Mr French was *splendid*!" said Ethel, "simply splendid."

Mr French stayed for lunch and spent the afternoon golfing with Ethel up at the links. And, as he walked down the drive much later with a smile on his lips and his mind flitting among the blissful memories of his afternoon with Ethel, an upper window was opened cautiously and a small head peeped out. Through the still air the words shot out, "*Two*, mind, an' with long tails."

"Where did you get it from?" demanded Mr Brown fiercely.

William pocketed his straying pet. "A friend gave it me."

"*What* friend?"

"Mr French. The man what carried me when I was took ill sudden. He gave me it. I di'n't know it was goin' to go into your slipper. An' I di'n't know it was goin' to bite your toe. It di'n't mean to bite your toe. I 'xpect it thought it was me givin' it sumthin' to eat. I expect—"

"Be *quiet*! What on earth did Mr French give you the confounded thing for?"

"I dunno. I 'xpect he jus' wanted to."

"How many of the wretched pests have you got?"

"They're rats," corrected William. "White 'uns. I've only got two."

"Good heavens! He's got *two*. Where's the other?"

"In the shed."

"Well *keep* it there, do you hear? And keep this savage brute out of the house as well . . ."

That night William obeyed the letter of the law by keeping the rats in the box on the sill outside his bedroom window.

The household was roused in the early hours of the morning by piercing screams from Ethel's room. The more adventurous of the pair – named Rufus – had escaped from the box and descended to Ethel's room by way of the creeper.

Ethel awoke suddenly to find it seated on her pillow, softly pawing her hair.

"Where *is* the wretched animal?" said Mr Brown a few minutes later, looking round with murder in his eyes.

"I've got it, Father," piped up William at the back of the crowd. "Ethel di'n't understand. It was playin' with her hair. It di'n't mean to frighten her. It—"

"I told you not to keep them in the house."

"They weren't in the house," said William firmly. "They were outside the window. Right on the sill. You can't call outside the window in the house, can you? I *put* it outside the house. I can't help it *comin'* inside the house when I'm asleep, can I?"

When Mr French called the next afternoon, he felt that his popularity had declined.

"I can't think why you gave William such dreadful things," Ethel said weakly, lying on the sofa. "I feel quite upset. And my nerves are a wreck, absolutely."

Mr French worked hard that afternoon and evening to regain his lost ground. In the drive he met William. William was holding a bloodstained handkerchief round his finger.

"It's bit me," he said indignantly. "One of those rats what you gave me's bit me."

Mr French looked at him apprehensively.

"You – you'd better not – er – tell your mother or sister about your finger. I – I wouldn't like your sister to be upset any more."

"What'll you give me not to?" said William.

Mr French plunged his hand into his pocket. "I'll give you half-a-crown," he said.

Things went well after that. Mr French arrived the next morning laden with flowers and grapes. The household unbent towards him. Ethel arranged a day's golfing with him.

Glorious vistas opened before William's eyes. He decided that Mr French must join the family. Life then would be an endless succession of half-crowns.

The next day was Sunday, and William went to the shed directly after breakfast to continue the teaching of Rufus, the dancing rat.

The other, now christened Cromwell, was to be taught to be friends with Jumble, William's dog. So far this training had only reached the point of Cromwell sitting motionless in the cage, while in front of it William violently restrained the enraged Jumble from murder. Still, William thought, if they looked at each other long enough, friendship would grow.

"William! It's time for church."

William groaned. He put Rufus in his

pocket and put the cage containing Cromwell on the top of a pile of boxes, leaving Jumble to continue the gaze of friendship from the floor.

He walked to church demurely behind his family, one hand clutching his prayer-book, the other in his pocket clasping Rufus. He hoped to be able to continue the training during the Litany.

It was during the hymn that the catastrophe occurred.

The Browns occupied the front pew of the church. While the second verse was being sung, the congregation was electrified by the sight of a small, long-tailed white creature appearing suddenly upon Mr Brown's shoulder.

Ethel's scream almost drowned the organ. Mr Brown put up his hand, and the intruder jumped upon his head and stood there for a second, digging his claws into his victim's scalp.

Mr Brown turned upon his son a purpled face that promised future vengeance. The choir turned fascinated eyes upon it, and the hymn died away.

William's face was a mask of horror.

Rufus next appeared running along the rim of the pulpit. The Vicar grew pale as Rufus approached and climbed up his reading-desk. A choirboy quickly grabbed it and retired into the vestry, and thence home before his right to its possession could be questioned.

William found his voice.

"He's took it," he said in a sibilant whisper. "It's mine! He took it!"

"*Ssh*!" said Ethel.

"It's mine. It's what Mr French give me for being took ill that day, you know."

"What?" said Ethel, leaning towards him. The hymn was in full swing again now.

"He gave it me for being took ill so's he could come and carry me home 'cause he was gone on you."

"*Ssh!*" hissed Mr Brown violently.

"I shall never look anyone in the face again," lamented Mrs Brown on the way home. "William, I don't know how you *could*!"

"Well, it's mine," said William. "That boy'd no business to take it. I di'n't *mean* it to get loose, an' get on Father's head an' scare folks. I meant it to be quiet, and stay in my pocket."

Ethel walked along with lips tightly shut. In the distance, walking towards them, was a tall, jaunty figure. It was Mr French, who, ignorant of what had happened, was coming gaily on to meet them returning from church. As Ethel approached he raised his hat with a flourish and beamed at her effusively.

Ethel walked past him, without a glance and with head high, leaving him, aghast and despairing, staring after her down the road.

William realised the situation. The future half-crowns seemed to vanish away.

"Ethel, don't get mad at Mr French. He only wanted to do sumthin' for you 'cause he

was mad on you."

"It's *horrible*," said Ethel. "First you bringing that dreadful animal to church, and then I find that he's deceived me, and you helped him. I hope Father takes the other rat away."

"He won't," said William. "He never said anything about that. The other's learning to be friends with Jumble in the shed. I say, Ethel, don't be mad at Mr French. He—"

"Oh, don't *talk* about him," said Ethel angrily.

William was something of a philosopher. "Well, I've got the other one left, anyway," he said.

They entered the drive and began to walk up to the front door. From the bushes Jumble dashed out to greet his master. His demeanour held more than ordinary pleasure. It expressed pride and triumph. At his master's feet he laid his proud offering – the mangled remains of Cromwell. William gasped.

"Oh, William!" said Ethel.

William assumed an expression of proud, restrained sorrow.

"All right!" he said generously. "It's not your fault really. An' it's not Jumble's fault. P'r'aps he thought it was what I was tryin' to teach him to do. It's jus' no one's fault. We'll have to bury it." His spirits rose. "I'll do the buryin' service out of the prayer-book."

He stood still gazing mournfully down at what was left of Jumble's friend. Jumble stood by it, proud and pleased, looking up with his head on one side and his tail wagging.

Sadly William reviewed the downfall of his hopes. Gone was Mr French and all he stood for. Gone was Rufus. Gone was Cromwell. He put his hand into his pocket, and it came in contact with the half-crown.

"Well," he said philosophically, "I've got *that* left anyway."

The
Old Man in the Fog

William wandered disconsolately about the crowded village hall looking, without much interest, at the various stalls, each laden with the useless articles that are characteristic of that peculiarly English institution, the Fête.

His mother had given him sixpence to spend and he had bought a packet of sweets at the home-made sweet stall, which had turned out to be so burnt that even he could not eat them.

He was just on the point of leaving in disgust, when he caught sight of a screen with a notice, "Fortune Teller", pinned on to it. It was tucked away in a small, unimportant-looking corner, and a small unimportant-looking woman sat nervously at a table inside.

She was beginning to suspect that it wasn't one of her Days. There were Days when she Could, and Days when she Couldn't, and this was, quite evidently, one of the Days when she Couldn't.

She saw William's head poked inquisitively round the edge of the screen and brightened. A boy. Surely a boy would be easy enough.

"Come in, my dear," she said. "It's two-and-six for a full reading."

"I've not got two-and-six," he said gloomily. "I've not got anything. I only had sixpence, and that's been stole off me. Well, I call it stealin', anyway. A dog couldn't 'ave et 'em." He handed her the paper bag. "Try if you can."

The fortune teller nervously refused.

"I don't mind anythin' a *bit* burnt," went on William expansively, "but these don't taste of anythin' but burnt. Not *anythin*'. I bet she *made* 'em of burnt. An' when you think what you could get for sixpence! Sixpence! Huh! I'd like to see her eat 'em herself."

The fortune teller looked at him speculatively. The boy was garrulous and ingenuous. He might prove useful. She cast her eye round the room for possible clients.

"Who's that pretty girl over there?" she said.

William's gloom deepened.

"Her?" he said. "Call *her* pretty? She's my sister, an' a jolly rotten sister she is, too. Wouldn't even give me a penny. Not a *penny*. An' she's got heaps of money. I bet she'll come along here in a minute to have her fortune told."

The fortune teller looked at Ethel again. She was quite the most attractive girl in the room. If she had her fortune told, and was pleased by it, probably everyone else would follow suit. She sympathised with William over the burnt sweets and began to chat with him.

William, touched by her interest, prattled volubly about his family and family affairs.

By the time that Ethel had decided to have her fortune told the fortune teller felt that she knew all about her that it was possible to know.

"*Said* she'd come," muttered William.

The fortune teller was naturally anxious that they should not meet.

"Go out at the back," she whispered to William, and pushed him out at the back of

63

the screen where it joined the wall.

It suddenly occurred to him to stop just out of sight and listen to Ethel's fortune.

He listened with growing amazement. Why, every single thing the fortune teller said was true. She even told Ethel that she'd sprained her thumb last week at Squash and that she'd been to a dance on Saturday. She told her that she was going away tomorrow night on a fortnight's visit to some friends in the North.

All this sounded so important and portentous, that William did not recognise it as part of his inconsequential chatter of a few moments ago, and was fully as impressed as Ethel herself.

William was just going to abandon his somewhat uncomfortable position when he saw that Robert had now entered.

The fortune teller began to ply Robert with artless questions, but Robert was determined to give nothing away and answered in monosyllables. The fortune teller sighed and bent over his hand.

"There's a legacy coming to you soon," she said. A legacy was always fairly safe. "Yes, a legacy. I see it plainly. A legacy. Have you any relative who's likely to leave you a legacy?"

"No," said Robert.

"Perhaps it's someone you've befriended."

"I've never befriended anyone," said Robert, uncompromisingly.

"Perhaps not knowingly," said the fortune teller, " but you may have befriended someone without realising it, out of sheer kindness of heart. I once knew a boy who helped an old man who was lost in the fog, and the old man left him all his fortune . . . As for your character," she went on, and William, who wasn't interested in Robert's character, stole softly away.

But William was intensely interested in Robert's legacy. He believed in it implicitly. Robert would soon be the possessor of a vast fortune, left to him by an old man whom he had once helped in a fog . . .

William could not resist dropping a few

"hints" here and there.

"Wait till Robert comes into his money," he said to Miss Bellfield when she deplored the unsatisfactory financial state of her Providence Club. "I bet he'll help you out."

Miss Bellfield gazed at him in astonishment. "What money?" she asked.

"Oh, this leg'cy of his."

"What legacy?"

"This leg'cy this ole man's leavin' him."

"What old man?"

"Well," explained William, "I don't know as he wants people to know, but he helped this ole man in a fog once, an' this ole man's leavin' him all his money."

"How does he know he is?"

"He told him. This ole man told him."

"People often say that, my dear boy, and forget to make a will."

"Oh, he's made a will, all right," said William airily. "An' it's all comin' to Robert. Every penny of it."

Miss Bellfield sighed. "Those are the people who go on living and living and living."

"He won't," said William. "He's dyin' now."

"How do you know?"

"They've sent word. He can't possibly live more'n' a week or two now."

"They've actually told Robert that he's the heir?"

"Yes."

"Dear me! How very interesting!"

William was feeling a little uneasy. The

67

main fact of the legacy, of course, was true enough (hadn't the fortune teller said so in so many words?) but, carried away by his imagination, he had added a few details that did not strictly conform to fact.

"Don't say anythin' to Robert about it," he said anxiously. "And p'raps you'd better not tell anyone else."

"Of course I won't, dear boy," said Miss Bellfield.

But, like William, she couldn't resist dropping a hint here and there, and by evening the whole village knew that Robert had been left an enormous fortune by an old man whom he had once helped in a fog, that the old man was lying on the point of death, and that his lawyer had formally notified Robert that he was the sole heir. In order to salve her conscience, she always added that Robert was anxious that no one should mention the subject to him.

Girls who had publicly announced they wouldn't marry Robert Brown if he was the last man in the world, hastily revised their views on the subject. But the legacy, though occasionally hinted at, was never actually mentioned to him.

Mrs Brown had been summoned to the sick bed of a sister, and Ethel had gone North on the prophesied visit, or they might, of course, have put an end to the misunderstanding.

As it was, Robert remained the courted idol of the neighbourhood. But it did not surprise him. For Robert had secretly purchased a book called, *How to be Popular.*

He'd at once set to work to study the book in the seclusion of his bedroom. It told him that he possessed secret powers of magnetism and attraction that only needed to be liberated. It hinted that, when the opposite sex should see him as he really was (dominating, irresistible, dynamic), it would fall for him in shoals. Robert didn't particularly want it to fall for him in shoals, but he did want Peggy Barlow to fall for him.

The rule that came over and over again was

"Hold up your Head and Look the World in the Face". Then you had to say to yourself: "I can if I will, not I will if I can." And: "Inexhaustible power surges within me."

Robert conscientiously committed these slogans to memory and sallied forth the next morning.

He was amazed by the instant success of the system. (It happened to be the day that the news of his legacy had spread through the village.) Everyone he spoke to (saying the little slogans to himself the while) gave him a new and respectful attention.

Peggy Barlow herself came down to the gate to meet him and, with a sweetness that made her almost unrecognisable, suggested a walk in the woods. During the walk she discoursed upon her utter indifference to wealth and luxury, and told him at least eleven times that she always liked people for themselves alone.

She repeated that money meant nothing to her, but nevertheless kept telling him how much she had always longed for a diamond brooch, a real pearl necklace and a high-powered motor car.

The fact that, at the end of the week, he won three pounds in a football pool, seemed to him only a natural part of his triumphant career. To William it was the fulfilment of the prophecy. Three pounds was, to him, untold wealth.

Anyway, he was glad that it had come at last. He walked through the village wearing an air of importance.

"Robert's got that money I told you about," he told everyone. "It came this morning."

The news spread like wildfire. Robert's legacy had arrived.

By evening, Robert had completely disposed of the three pounds. He had bought a pair of tyres for his motorcycle, given a shilling to William, and spent the remaining five shillings on a present for Peggy. It was, he considered, an extremely handsome present – a large paste brooch, in the shape of a motor car. The Mercers were giving a party that night, and he meant to present it to her then. He looked forward with pleasure to her gratitude.

Strange to remember how aloof and disdainful she had been only a short time ago. His liberated dynamic personality had made a completely different person of her.

He and William set out together, Robert silent and aloof.

"I can if I will," he murmured to himself as he went along. "Inexhaustible power surges within me."

William, on his side, was feeling at peace with himself and all the world. There would be jellies, blancmanges and trifles; and Robert had come into his money, so that episode was satisfactorily closed.

Peggy Barlow was waiting for Robert just inside the dance-room. Robert took her to an alcove and pressed the little packet into her hands.

"Just a small present," he explained.

Peggy opened it.

"Oh, Robert!" she gasped. "*Diamonds*!"

Robert laughed. "Well, hardly *diamonds* exactly, but they do get them up awfully well, nowadays, don't they?"

Peggy stared at him. "Do you mean they aren't *real*?"

Robert's mouth dropped open. "How on *earth* do you think I could buy real diamonds?"

"You got your money this morning, didn't you?"

"Yes," said Robert, "but—"

She interrupted angrily. "And you bring me a cheap thing like this!"

"Hang it all! It cost five shillings. I don't call *that* cheap."

"Five *shillings*! Five *shillings*! You got all that money this morning, and you spend five shillings on me."

"It was a jolly sight more than I could afford, too," said Robert.

"You're going to be *very* careful of it, aren't you?" sneered Peggy.

"I don't know what you call careful," said Robert. "I've spent it all, anyway. It was three pounds."

"Three—?"

"Yes. Three pounds from one of those football pools."

"But what about your legacy?" she said.

"Legacy? What legacy?"

"The legacy from the old man in the fog?"

"The – the *what*?"

"The old man in the fog. The one you found lost and showed the way to, and who left you his fortune."

Robert looked bewildered. "I don't know what you're talking about. You must be thinking of someone else."

Peggy stamped angrily. "Of *course* I'm not thinking of anyone else. You spread this story just to get me to take some notice of you and then you have the nerve to stand there and tell me that it was all a deliberate lie."

Robert felt that he must be dreaming. "Listen! I never told you about any old man in a fog."

"No," agreed Peggy contemptuously, "you were too much of a skunk even to do that. You got someone else to do your dirty work. You spread the story through an innocent child. *Oh!*"

With that she turned on her heel and left him. He stared after her. She must have gone mad. Well, he didn't care. And he'd just show her too. Clarinda Bellew, Dolly Clavis and Cornelia Gerrard had been pestering him for dances all the week. He approached Clarinda and asked her for a dance. But already the report was flying round the room. Robert Brown hadn't got any legacy, after all. He'd only won three pounds in a football pool and, what was more, already spent it.

Clarinda looked at him disdainfully and said that her programme was full. Dazedly, he passed on to Dolly Clavis. Dolly Clavis didn't even bother to speak to him.

Robert struggled to collect his forces. This was a crisis. He'd forgotten to say the little slogans since he entered the dance hall and this was the result. He stood quite still, and said them over to himself then, grimly controlled, he approached Honoria Mercer.

"Have you a dance for me, Honoria?" (I can if I will. I can if I will. Inexhaustible power surges within me.)

Honoria gave a nasty, sarcastic laugh and turned on her heel.

Robert faced final failure. The slogans had

ceased to work.

People passed him haughtily, contemptuously, with averted faces. There was no getting away from the fact that the slogans had failed. But, surely, there was more than that to it. What had Peggy said about an old man in a fog? What she said about an *innocent child*?

Innocent child . . . The more he thought of it, the more certain he was that *William* was at the bottom of it.

He looked around the room. William was nowhere to be seen, but Robert knew where he'd be. With firm and measured tread, he set off in the direction of the supper-room. An inexhaustible power surged within him . . .

Meet Just William
Adapted by Martin Jarvis
Illustrated by Tony Ross

Just William as you've never seen him before.

A wonderful new series of *Just William* books, each containing
four of his funniest stories – all specially adapted for younger
readers by Martin Jarvis, the famous "voice of William" on radio
and best-selling audio cassette.

Meet Just William and the long-suffering Brown family, as well as
the Outlaws, Violet Elizabeth Bott and a host of other favourite
characters in these six hilarious books.

Richmal Crompton
Just William and Other Animals

*"You can't have another dog, William," said Mrs Brown firmly,
"you've got one."*
"Well it's at the vet's an' I want a dog to be going on with."

William has a certain affinity with members of the animal kingdom.
In fact, some would say that William is rather like his furry friends.
And he would do anything to help an animal in distress (unless it's
a cat).

Champion of canine causes, defender of innocent rodents,
avenger of bestial wrongs – no tormentor of rats or pups is safe
when William Brown is around . . .

Ten classic stories of William – and other animals.

"Probably the funniest, toughest children's books ever written"
Sunday Times

Richmal Crompton
Just William at Christmas

Christmas is a time for peace, joy and goodwill. But William's presence has never been known to enhance the spirit of the season.

Whether he's wrecking the Sunday School's carol singing outing, standing in as Santa Claus for the Old Folk, or making a Christmas plant pot out of Ethel's hat, William somehow manages to spread chaos wherever he goes.

Ten unforgettable stories of William at Christmas, with the original illustrations by Thomas Henry.

Richmal Crompton
Just William at School

*"School's not nat'ral at all," said William. "Still, I don't suppose
they'd let us give it up altogether, 'cause of schoolmasters havin'
to have something to do."*

School is fertile ground for a boy of William's infinite trouble-
making talent. Especially when he'd rather not be there at all.
Whether he's feigning illness to avoid a test, campaigning for the
abolition of Latin and Arithmetic, or breaking into Ole Fathead's
house in pursuit of justice, William brings muddle and mayhem to
anyone who tries to teach him a lesson.

Ten classic stories of William at school – and trying desperately to
get out of it!

Richmal Crompton
Just Jimmy

"I'm not a kid," Jimmy said stoutly. *"I'm seven and three-quarters and four d-days and a n-night."*

Meet Jimmy Manning – a boy in a hurry to grow up, especially if it means he can join his brother Roger's gang, the Three Musketeers.

Whether he's waging war on arch-enemies the Mouldies, plotting to catch criminals with his best friend Bobby Peaslake, or fighting off the attentions of the dreaded Araminta, Jimmy's plans are always ingenious, hilarious – and destined for disaster!

First published in 1949 and lost for decades, *Just Jimmy* is a rediscovered classic from the creator of *Just William*.

Collect all the titles in the
MEET JUST WILLIAM series!

The prices shown below are correct at the time of going to press. However, Macmillan Publishers reserve the right to show new retail prices on covers which may differ from those previously advertised.

William's Birthday	0 330 39097 X	£2.99
William and the Hidden Treasure	0 330 39100 3	£2.99
William's Wonderful Plan	0 330 39102 X	£2.99
William and the Prize Cat	0 330 39098 8	£2.99
William and the Haunted House	0 330 39101 1	£2.99
William's Day Off	0 330 39099 6	£2.99
William and the White Elephants	0 330 39210 7	£2.99
William and the School Report	0 330 39210 7	£2.99
William's Midnight Adventure	0 330 39212 3	£2.99
William's Busy Day	0 330 39213 1	£2.99

All *Meet Just William* titles can be ordered at your local bookshop or are available by post from:

Book Service by Post
PO Box 29, Douglas, Isle of Man IM99 1BQ

Credit cards accepted. For details:
Telephone: 01624 675137
Fax: 01624 670923
E-mail: bookshop@enterprise.net

Free postage and packing in the UK.
Overseas customers: add £1 per book (paperback)
and £3 per book (hardback).